KATE'S *REALLY* GOOD AT
HOCKEY

animalmediagroup.com

Written by Christina M. Frey &
Howard Shapiro

Illustrated by Jade Gonzalez

Colors by Liezl Buenaventura

Lettered by Saida Temofonte

Animal Media Group, LLC
Pittsburgh

Kate's Really Good at Hockey
Copyright © 2018 by Christina M. Frey and Howard Shapiro

Animal Media Group books may be ordered through booksellers or by contacting:

Animal Media Group
100 1st Ave. Suite 1100
Pittsburgh, PA 15222

www.animalmediagroup.com
412-566-5656

Animal Media Group is distributed by
Consortium Book Sales & Distribution Co.

ISBN: 978-1-947895-06-5 (pblc)
ISBN: 978-1-947895-07-2 (eblc)

CHAPTER 1

LET ME GUESS...

...SOMETHING TO DO WITH...

HOCKEY!

WELL, I MEAN...

...SORT OF...

IT STARTED THE DAY I GOT THE LETTER--

--THE LETTER FROM THE NORTH AMERICAN WOMEN'S ICE HOCKEY FEDERATION. THEY HOLD A SIX-WEEK DEVELOPMENTAL CAMP IN DENVER, COLORADO, FOR ELITE JUNIOR GIRLS AGES TEN TO THIRTEEN FROM ALL OVER THE WORLD.

IT'S VERY DIFFICULT TO GET AN INVITE TO THE CAMP. YOU HAVE TO FILL OUT A LONG APPLICATION AND SEND IN VIDEO HIGHLIGHTS AND RECOMMENDATIONS.

HAVING MAD HOCKEY SKILLS ISN'T ENOUGH.

YOU NEED TO BE SOMEONE WHO LIVES AND BREATHES HOCKEY--

--AND THAT'S ME! HOCKEY HAS BEEN MY LIFE, TWENTY-FOUR SEVEN, FOR AS LONG AS I CAN REMEMBER.

KRISH

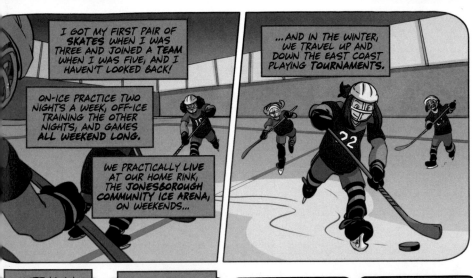

I GOT MY FIRST PAIR OF SKATES WHEN I WAS THREE AND JOINED A TEAM WHEN I WAS FIVE, AND I HAVEN'T LOOKED BACK!

ON-ICE PRACTICE TWO NIGHTS A WEEK, OFF-ICE TRAINING THE OTHER NIGHTS, AND GAMES ALL WEEKEND LONG.

WE PRACTICALLY LIVE AT OUR HOME RINK, THE JONESBOROUGH COMMUNITY ICE ARENA, ON WEEKENDS...

...AND IN THE WINTER, WE TRAVEL UP AND DOWN THE EAST COAST PLAYING TOURNAMENTS.

GETTING AN INVITE TO THE DEVELOPMENTAL CAMP IN DENVER MEANT THE WORLD TO ME!

TO BE THE BEST, YOU HAVE TO COMPETE AGAINST THE BEST...

...AND THAT'S WHAT I WANT TO DO!

I APPLIED FOR THE CAMP...

...AND THEN CAME THE WAITING.

AND WAITING.

AND WAITING!!

AH....!

MOM!!✦

READY, SET--

I DON'T KNOW IF THIS IS SUCH A GOOD IDEA, MOM.

THINK POSITIVE THOUGHTS, HONEY.

WELL, HERE GOES NOTHING.

...

WHAT DOES IT SAY? IT'S ALL RIGHT IF IT'S A NO.

I'M PROUD OF YOUR HARD WORK. I'VE ALWAYS SAID--

I KNOW. "YOU DON'T HAVE TO BE THE BEST PLAYER ON THE ICE, BUT YOU SHOULD BE THE **BEST** AT **OUTWORKING** EVERY OTHER PLAYER THERE."

BUT MOM, DO YOU THINK...

...WHAT IF THE OTHER GIRLS ARE REALLY GOOD?

OF COURSE THEY'LL BE GOOD! THAT'LL HELP **YOU** UP YOUR GAME.

YOU'LL TACKLE THE CHALLENGE LIKE YOU ALWAYS DO.

BESIDES, NO ONE THERE IS AS **DEDICATED** AS YOU ARE...

CHAPTER 2

THE MINUTE I FOUND OUT I'D BEEN ACCEPTED INTO CAMP, I WAS ON IT.

SHUFFLE

I PRACTICED HARDER THAN EVER.

≷HUFF≷
≷HUFF≷

I WATCHED REPLAYS OF MY BEST GAMES...AND MY WORST GAMES, TOO.

I CRACKED DOWN ON HOMEWORK AFTER MOM WARNED ME THAT "A FAILING GRADE IS A ONE-WAY TICKET TO SUMMER SCHOOL."

SCRIBBLE SCRIBBLE

I EVEN GOT A HEAD START ON PACKING!

KNOCK
KNOCK

SO...?

THE GOOD NEWS IS THAT YOU DON'T NEED ALL THAT.

...

UM.

UH.

I JUST GOT OFF THE PHONE WITH GRANDMA...

...AND SHE SAYS YOU CAN *STAY WITH HER* IN DENVER.

WHAT? BUT I THOUGHT...

WE DIDN'T WANT TO SAY ANYTHING UNTIL WE KNEW FOR SURE.

SHE'S *VERY* EXCITED!

BUT WE *TALKED* ABOUT IT! I CAN STAY IN THE *DORMS* OR WHEREVER THE *OTHER GIRLS* AT CAMP ARE--

NO, YOU CAN STAY WITH YOUR *GRANDMOTHER.* SHE LIVES FIFTEEN MINUTES FROM THE ARENA COMPLEX.

IT WILL MAKE HER SO HAPPY--

BUT MOM, I *HARDLY* KNOW GRANDMA. SHE'S VISITED HERE, WHAT, LIKE *TWICE?*

SHE WAS HERE SIX MONTHS AGO.

I COULDN'T BELIEVE THEY'D ALREADY DECIDED... WITHOUT ME.

CAMP WAS A HUGE OPPORTUNITY. I NEEDED TO STAY *FOCUSED*. AND GRANDMA-- SHE WOULDN'T UNDERSTAND.

AND THE SUMMER BEFORE THAT, AND TWICE A YEAR SINCE YOU WERE BORN.

AND WE VISITED HER TWO YEARS AGO.

OH RIGHT, THE TIME WHEN DUSTIN--

NOT *TODAY*, KATE.

AND HER TINY TV WAS BROKEN AND THERE WAS NO WI-FI AND WE COULDN'T GET A CELL SIGNAL AND IT WAS THE *WORST*--

KATE, *PLEASE*!

AND YOU WILL *NOT* BE USING YOUR PHONE WHILE YOU SPEND TIME WITH YOUR GRANDMOTHER! YOU CAN TRY TALKING--

I CAN'T *TALK* TO HER ABOUT ANYTHING! ALL SHE DOES IS READ BOOKS AND WORK IN HER GARDEN. AND I...

WHAT'S GOTTEN INTO YOU? THIS ISN'T LIKE YOU AT ALL. YOU'LL STAY WITH YOUR GRANDMOTHER...

...AND THAT'S FINAL.

HMPF.

MOM WAS RIGHT, KIND OF. AND IT WASN'T ABOUT THE WI-FI...

...ALTHOUGH, YOU KNOW...

DEVELOPMENTAL CAMP COULD CHANGE MY LIFE.

AND MY GRANDMA...

WELL, LAST TIME SHE VISITED, I HAD A TOURNAMENT, AND SHE NEVER EVEN ASKED ABOUT IT.

NOT EVEN WHEN I SHOWED HER MY MUP TROPHY!

SHE'S NEVER BEEN TO ANY OF MY GAMES. OR TALKED TO ME ABOUT HOCKEY AT ALL.

I TOLD HER I WANTED TO BE THE FIRST GIRL IN THE CAHL-- THE CAN-AM HOCKEY LEAGUE--

--AND GO UP AGAINST MY HERO, JEREMIAH JACOBSON...

...AND SHE SAID NOTHING!

SHE DIDN'T COME WITH ME AND DAD TO WATCH GAME ONE OF THE COVA CUP FINALS, AND HER HOME TEAM WAS PLAYING!

I TOLD MOM I DIDN'T KNOW GRANDMA AT ALL...

CHAPTER 3

BYE...

...

SO... LOOKING FORWARD TO CAMP?

OH YEAH! TWO DAYS!

I COULDN'T BELIEVE GRANDMA HAD ASKED ME ABOUT HOCKEY!

DID MOM TELL YOU? THIS IS LIKE THE **BEST GIRLS' HOCKEY CAMP** IN THE WORLD! EVERYONE THERE WILL BE AT A **SUPER-ELITE** LEVEL...

...AND I CAN'T WAIT FOR THE **CHALLENGE.** I'LL GO UP AGAINST GIRLS FROM RUSSIA, JAPAN, ECUADOR, INDIA, AND... I FORGET THE REST!

THIS IS THE FIRST STEP IN MY HOCKEY MASTER PLAN. IN A FEW YEARS, I'M GOING TO BE THE **FIRST GIRL** IN THE **MINORS**...

...AND THEN THE **FIRST GIRL** IN THE **CAHL**...

...AND I'LL PLAY AGAINST MY **HERO,** JEREMIAH JACOBSON.

THAT'S **MY PLAN,** AND I'M STICKING TO IT!

AND IT ALL STARTS WITH **KILLING IT** HERE AT **CAMP.**

OKAY. GOOD.

WE HAD **NOTHING** IN COMMON.

I'M HUNGRY. WANT TO GO GET **ICE CREAM?**

SURE!

OKAY, ONE THING IN COMMON.

ONE HOUR LATER...

AFTER ICE CREAM-- COTTON CANDY FLAVOR, MY FAVORITE--WE WENT TO THE GROCERY STORE TO STOCK UP.

EXCEPT THAT THE FOOD GRANDMA WANTED TO STOCK UP ON, WELL...

OH, UM...

I'M SORRY, HONEY. I'M SO USED TO GETTING THE SAME THINGS THAT I NEGLECTED TO ASK YOU WHAT *YOU'D LIKE* TO EAT.

WHY DON'T YOU TOSS IN WHAT YOU USUALLY BUY?

WELL, SINCE I'LL BE IN TRAINING, I'LL NEED A *LOT*. PASTA, SWEET POTATOES, AND BROWN AND WILD RICE FOR A START.

AND LET'S SEE, I'LL ALSO NEED SOME *PROTEIN* LIKE WHITE-MEAT CHICKEN, TURKEY, AND HAMBURGERS.

AND GUAC AND SOY SAUCE. THEN SOME *VEGETABLES* AND BLUEBERRIES AND LOTS OF EGGS, AND MILK AND CEREAL AND...

AFTER WE GOT HOME AND PUT THE GROCERIES AWAY, GRANDMA SAID WE SHOULD COOK DINNER TOGETHER--THAT IT WOULD HELP US GET TO KNOW EACH OTHER.

TRY TO CONNECT WITH GRANDMA, OKAY, KATE? EVEN IF IT'S HARD, IT'S WORTH THE EFFORT. TRUST ME.

SO, UM, YOU LIKE GARDENING, RIGHT?

YES, BUT...

...I WON'T BE PUTTING IN A GARDEN THIS YEAR.

OHH...

THAT WAS AWKWARD.

HOW'S SCHOOL GOING?

I GUESS IT WENT OKAY. BUT IT'S SUMMER VACATION, SO--

NO SUMMER SCHOOL?

SUMMER SCHOOL??

WELL, NO. I'M FOCUSING ON THE HOCKEY CAMP THIS SUMMER. IT'S A *HUGE* OPPORTUNITY TO UP MY GAME.

HOCKEY IS FINE, KATE, BUT YOU HAVE TO FOCUS ON YOUR *STUDIES*, TOO. THAT'S THE *IMPORTANT* THING. BEFORE YOU KNOW IT, *COLLEGE* WILL BE RIGHT AROUND THE CORNER. AND THEN...

SO IS *THAT* HER DEAL? SHE THINKS I SHOULD BE STUDYING FOR COLLEGE INSTEAD OF PLAYING *HOCKEY*?

...

I HAD THIS **AWESOME SOCIAL STUDIES** TEACHER, AND SHE TOLD US TO FIND **SOMETHING WE LOVE** DOING AND **WORK REALLY HARD** AT IT. FOR ME, THAT'S **HOCKEY.** I'M ALL IN TO MAKE IT MY CAREER.

EVEN IF I DON'T MAKE THE CAHL--AS IF **THAT'S** POSSIBLE--I'LL STILL DO SOMETHING IN HOCKEY. LIKE BEING A **COACH!** SO I CAN USE THE SKILLS THEN TOO, EVEN IF I'M NOT PLAYING.

OH, I SEE.

CLINK

CLINK

THIS IS IMPOSSIBLE.

BUT I WAS SUPER NERVOUS ABOUT MONDAY. CAMP WAS MY CHANCE TO PROVE MYSELF AGAINST THE BEST...

...SO I NEEDED TO LEARN AS MUCH AS I COULD AND WORK HARD TO IMPRESS THE COACHES.

AND I WAS DESPERATE TO TALK ABOUT IT WITH SOMEONE WHO'D GET IT. OR WHO AT LEAST WANTED TO TRY.

KATE?

ASK ME ABOUT TOMORROW, ASK ME ABOUT TOMORROW...

WELL, I'M PRETTY BEAT, AND SIX O'CLOCK IN THE MORNING COMES AROUND AWFULLY EARLY. I GUESS I'LL SAY GOOD NIGHT.

GOOD NIGHT, GRANDMA.

CHAPTER 4

AND WITH THAT, IT WAS GAME ON: SKATING WITH NO BREAK FOR NINETY MINUTES STRAIGHT. WHEN WE GOT OFF THE ICE, I THOUGHT I WAS GOING TO PUKE.

FIIII

WE WERE BACK ON THE ICE AFTER LUNCH.

THEN RUNNING LAPS.

I'D NEVER WORKED SO HARD IN MY LIFE!

≥PANT≥

≥AUFF≥

THEN, AFTER PRACTICE, COACH THATCHER CAME INTO THE LOCKER ROOM AND STARTED THROWING SHADE.

ANYA, I HOPE YOUR STICKHANDLING AND YOUR AIM ARE BETTER THAN YOUR SKATING. I NEED TO SEE MORE OUT OF YOU, FULL STOP.

NAYELI, NOT BAD TODAY BUT DEFINITELY NOT WHAT I EXPECTED TO SEE. YOU HAVE A WAYS TO GO WITH YOUR FOOTWORK.

STRONG SKATERS ARE GOOD PLAYERS, PRISHA. IF YOU WANT TO BE A SHUTDOWN DEFENDER, I'LL NEED TO SEE BETTER FOOTWORK FROM HERE ON OUT.

LADIES, I SPENT MY CHILDHOOD WATCHING YOUR GRANDFATHER, PIE LACROIX, AND IF HE WERE HERE HE'D AGREE WITH ME: YOU THREE NEED TO BRING A LOT MORE TO THE RINK TOMORROW THAN YOU DID TODAY.

KATE KAZMEIER. I HEARD YOU WERE THE SECOND COMING OF HAYLEY WICKENHEISER.

WHAT I SAW OUT THERE WASN'T EVEN CLOSE. BRING YOUR A-GAME TOMORROW. GOT IT?

YES, COACH THATCHER.

I **RECOGNIZED** YOU IMMEDIATELY. WE **BEAT** YOU GUYS IN THE BEAST OF THE EAST TOURNAMENT IN PITTSBURGH LAST YEAR.

WHO CARES? OUR WORST PLAYER IN DRUMMONDVILLE COULD **SKATE CIRCLES** AROUND YOU.

I THINK YOU HAVE ME MIXED UP WITH SOMEONE ELSE. I'VE NEVER PLAYED IN PITTSBURGH, AND I CAN GUARANTEE I WOULD REMEMBER PLAYING AGAINST YOU.

WHERE ARE YOU FROM?

TENNESSEE, AND WE HAVE SOME PRETTY GOOD HOCKEY PLAYERS THERE.

TENNESSEE? ARE YOU **SERIOUS?** THERE ARE **NO** GOOD HOCKEY PLAYERS FROM TENNESSEE. YOU WOULDN'T LAST ONE DAY IN QUEBEC, LITTLE GIRL.

WHY DON'T YOU JUST LEAVE HER ALONE AND GET CHANGED. IT WAS A *TOUGH PRACTICE,* AND COACH THATCHER--

SAYS THE GIRL FROM *WHERE?* WHAT'S YOUR NAME *AGAIN?*

NAYELI. I'M FROM QUITO, ECUADOR.

THAT'S JUST GREAT, NAYELI FROM QUITO, *ECUADOR.* MAYBE THE ONLY WORSE PLACE TO PLAY HOCKEY THAN *TENNESSEE.* DO YOU EVEN HAVE *ICE* IN ECUADOR? MAYBE TO PUT IN YOUR *PEPSI!*

CLAP

LET'S GO, JOCELYN, SARAH.

THANK YOU FOR, YOU KNOW, STICKING UP FOR ME.

MY *COACH* BACK HOME TAUGHT ME NOT TO PICK FIGHTS, BUT NOT TO *RUN AWAY* FROM ONE, EITHER.

AND I DIDN'T COME ALL THIS WAY TO BE *BULLIED* BY THOSE GIRLS OR *ANYONE* ELSE.

WE HAVE A PRETTY SMALL BUT CLOSE-KNIT HOCKEY COMMUNITY IN QUITO, AND THEY KNEW IT WAS MY *DREAM* TO COME HERE AND TEST MYSELF AGAINST THE BEST.

MY TEAM AND OUR WHOLE COMMUNITY RAISED THE *MONEY* TO ALLOW ME TO COME HERE. I'M GOING TO DO THEM *PROUD.*

SLAM

THAT'S AWESOME!

AS YOU HEARD, I'M *KATE* FROM TENNESSEE.

GREAT TO OFFICIALLY MEET YOU, KATE FROM TENNESSEE. AS YOU KNOW, I'M *NAYELI* FROM *QUITO,* ECUADOR.

WHERE ICE IS ONLY FOR SODA, NOT TO SKATE ON.

HA HAHA

SEE YOU TOMORROW!

CHAPTER 5

I WENT INTO DAY TWO OF CAMP THINKING IT COULDN'T BE ANY TOUGHER THAN DAY ONE. WAS I EVER WRONG!

THAT FIRST HOUR-- AGAIN, NOT A PUCK IN SIGHT. SKATING AND MORE SKATING.

BREAK TIME! BACK OUT HERE IN TWENTY!

GOOD JOB OUT THERE, LADIES.

WHAT WAS THAT ALL ABOUT?

THE FIRST DRILLS WERE TWO-ON-TWO BATTLES. WE HAD TO SCORE THREE GOALS TO WIN.

THE LOSING TWOSOME HAD TO SKATE FROM END TO END TWICE, AT FULL SPEED.

TIME TO SHOW COACH THATCHER WHAT I'M ALL ABOUT.

NAYELI AND I WERE UP AGAINST JOCELYN AND SARAH LACROIX. JUST OUR LUCK.

LET'S SHOW THESE TWO PRETENDERS HOW WE DO IT IN QUEBEC.

TOCK

CRUNCH

CHUFF

HEY!!

COACH, THAT GOAL SHOULDN'T COUNT! THAT WAS INTERFERENCE!

IT'S CALLED PUCK AWARENESS, KATE. IF YOU WANT TO BE A SOLID ALL-AROUND PLAYER, YOU'RE GOING TO NEED IT.

PRISHA, CAYLA, TAMAR, ANYA, YOU'RE UP NEXT.

KATE, NAYELI, TWO LAPS AT FULL SPEED.

BUT COACH, IT WAS INTERFERENCE. SHE BLOCKED ME FROM GETTING THE PUCK. A REFEREE WOULD--

YOU WANT TO MAKE IT FOUR LAPS, KATE?

COME ON, KATE. WE LOST, SO LET'S JUST DO OUR LAPS.

I BET I CAN BEAT YOU!

IT'S NOT FAIR.

THAT WAS INTERFERENCE.

PUCK AWARENESS. COACH THATCHER SHOULD HAVE BEEN PAYING BETTER ATTENTION.

THINGS DIDN'T GET BETTER AFTER THAT.

HMPF.

SMIRK

MY GAME WAS OFF.

I MADE STUPID MISTAKES.

KATE! GET YOUR HEAD BACK IN THE GAME!

COMPETITION *TOO FIERCE* FOR YOU, LITTLE GIRL?

YOU DON'T STAND A CHANCE WITH US!

WELL, IF YOU--

SHE'S JUST TRYING TO MESS WITH YOU.

WHAT SHE DID THIS MORNING WAS ILLEGAL! IT WAS INTERFERENCE!

I KNOW THAT AND YOU KNOW THAT, AND JOCELYN AND SARAH KNOW IT, TOO.

BUT IT'S TIME TO MOVE ON.

THEY GOT AWAY WITH IT. COACH THATCHER LET THEM.

WELL, SHE LET IT SLIDE, ANYWAY, AND WE CAN'T DO ANYTHING ABOUT IT. WE'LL COME BACK TOMORROW AND SHOW THEM WHAT WE'VE GOT.

CHAPTER 6

HEY, RELAX, KATE. AT LEAST WE WON'T BE UP AGAINST THOSE TWO TODAY.

SWISH

IT.

WAS.

ON.

I FIGURED JOCELYN WAS GOING TO COME STRAIGHT AFTER ME, SO BEFORE COACH THATCHER WHISTLED US TO START, I TOLD NAYELI TO GO TO THE FRONT OF THE NET.

PUCK AWARENESS-- THINK WHERE THE PUCK IS *GOING*, NOT WHERE IT'S AT.

I'D GO INTO THE CORNER FIRST.

I KNEW SHE WAS GUNNING FOR ME. BUT IF SHE WAS GOING TO CHECK ME AGAIN...

... I'D BE READY.

KRR

TAK

GRIN

IF JOCELYN LACROIX COULD PLAY DIRTY, THEN WHY COULDN'T I? IT WAS ONLY FAIR.

COACH THATCHER WAS PICKING ON ME, BUT JOCELYN WAS THE ONE GETTING AWAY WITH EVERYTHING.

KATE...

AND I WASN'T GOING TO STAND FOR IT.

HMM...

COACH

COACH, THERE'S SOMETHING YOU NEED TO KNOW, BECAUSE I DON'T THINK I WAS TREATED *FAIRLY* OUT THERE. JOCELYN--

I DIDN'T TREAT YOU *FAIRLY?* DID YOU OR DID YOU *NOT* SLEW-FOOT JOCELYN LACROIX TODAY?

I... THAT'S NOT--

IT DIDN'T QUITE WORK OUT THAT WAY.

I THOUGHT IF I COULD JUST *EXPLAIN* WHAT WAS GOING ON TO COACH THATCHER, SHE'D AGREE THAT JOCELYN HAD *DESERVED* IT.

DID YOU OR DID YOU *NOT?*

YES, OKAY. BUT ONLY BECAUSE--

YOU'RE VERY TALENTED, BUT I'VE SEEN PLAYERS LIKE YOU *COME* AND *GO* OVER THE YEARS. *THE HOTSHOTS* WHO ACT ENTITLED BECAUSE THEY HAVE SOME TALENT. THEN THEY DON'T GET *THEIR WAY,* AND THEY ASSUME THE WORLD'S AGAINST THEM.

IF YOU WANT TO *WORK HARD* ON THE ICE AND OFF, NO EXCUSES, THEN I'LL SEE YOU TOMORROW.

IF NOT, HAVE A SAFE TRIP BACK TO *TENNESSEE.*

YOU COULD HAVE SERIOUSLY INJURED HER. YOU WANT TO BE TREATED FAIRLY? YOU'RE *LUCKY* I'M GIVING YOU A CHANCE TO COME BACK TOMORROW.

"BUT COACH THATCHER--"

"THIS CONVERSATION IS OVER, KATE."

I COULDN'T BELIEVE IT. JOCELYN WAS THE ENTITLED HOTSHOT--AND SHE WAS A *BULLY,* TOO. AND IT WASN'T JUST COACH THATCHER WHO TOOK JOCELYN'S SIDE.

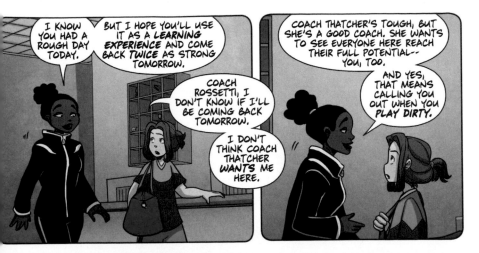

I KNOW YOU HAD A ROUGH DAY TODAY.

BUT I HOPE YOU'LL USE IT AS A *LEARNING EXPERIENCE* AND COME BACK *TWICE* AS STRONG TOMORROW.

COACH ROSSETTI, I DON'T KNOW IF I'LL BE COMING BACK TOMORROW.

I DON'T THINK COACH THATCHER *WANTS* ME HERE.

COACH THATCHER'S TOUGH, BUT SHE'S A GOOD COACH. SHE WANTS TO SEE EVERYONE HERE REACH THEIR FULL POTENTIAL-- YOU, TOO.

AND YES, THAT MEANS CALLING YOU OUT WHEN YOU *PLAY DIRTY.*

BUT JOCELYN--

KATE, I KNOW YOU'RE A BETTER PLAYER THAN THAT. YOU'RE A BETTER *PERSON* THAN THAT.

SO PUT THIS BEHIND YOU AND *MOVE FORWARD.* YOU OWE IT TO YOURSELF--AND TO YOUR TEAMMATES, TOO.

AND THAT INCLUDES JOCELYN LACROIX.

HELLO, COACH.

READY TO GO, KATE?

I SURE AM.

CHAPTER 7

SO, ARE YOU GOING TO TALK ABOUT IT...

... OR JUST SIT THERE AND STEW?

THE COACH *HATES* ME, THERE ARE TWO *CRAZED LUNATICS* LOOKING TO CHEAP-SHOT ME EVERY TIME I TOUCH THE PUCK, AND... THE COACH *REALLY HATES* ME.

BOTH COACHES HATE ME.

SO YOU'RE JUST GOING TO TAKE YOUR HOCKEY STICK AND GO *HOME?*

YEP.

I SEE.

GRANDMA WASN'T ON MY SIDE EITHER. NO SURPRISE THERE.

STUFF
STUFF

YOU SEEM VERY SURE ABOUT THIS.

I AM.

I THINK YOU'D BEST STAY AND COMPETE.

HOW DO YOU EXPECT TO GO UP AGAINST JEREMIAH JACOBSON OR PLAY IN THE CAHL IF *YOU QUIT* WHEN THE *GOING GETS TOUGH?*

WAIT. SHE WAS LISTENING?

MAYBE GRANDMA HAD A POINT, BUT THIS WASN'T ABOUT THE GOING GETTING TOUGH. NAYELI AND PRISHA AND THE OTHER GIRLS MADE IT FUN. AND I KNEW THE DRILLS COULD IMPROVE MY SKILL SET--

--BUT HOW COULD I PLAY MY BEST GAME IF I HAD TO SPEND THE WHOLE TIME WATCHING MY BACK?

I *TRIED* TO PUT A STOP TO JOCELYN'S BULLYING, AND COACH THATCHER SHUT ME DOWN.

COACH WASN'T GOING TO DO *ANYTHING* ABOUT IT, AND IF I DIDN'T LIKE IT, I COULD LEAVE.

IT WASN'T FAIR FOR GRANDMA TO ASSUME I WAS A QUITTER.

LET'S HAVE DINNER FIRST. NO GOOD MAKING A BIG DECISION ON AN EMPTY STOMACH.

...

YOU KNOW, I'M IN THE MOOD FOR SOMETHING *DIFFERENT.* WILL YOU RUN DOWN TO THE BASEMENT...

...AND GRAB A JAR OF SPAGHETTI SAUCE?

LEFT OF THE STAIRS, FOURTH SHELF FROM THE BOTTOM, RIGHT-HAND SIDE, TOWARD THE BACK.

GOT IT.

CREAK

TOMATOES, PICKLES, SALSA--WAIT, SHE HAS...

...SALSA?

SHE MUST HAVE MEANT A DIFFERENT SHELF. THERE'S NO SPAGHETTI--

--SAUCE?!

CHAPTER 8

WHIZZZ

GUESS WE DIDN'T NEED THAT PASTA SAUCE AFTER ALL.

JOSEPHINE CAMERON, MVP. JOSEPHINE CAMERON, ALL-STAR GOALIE. ALL-STAR? I DIDN'T EVEN *KNOW* YOU PLAYED *HOCKEY!*

HONEY, IT FEELS LIKE THAT WAS *TWO* LIFETIMES AGO.

BUT... I THOUGHT YOU... WHY *DIDN'T...*?

WHY DIDN'T I TELL YOU I PLAYED HOCKEY?

SHE DIDN'T JUST PLAY HOCKEY, SHE WAS *THE BEST!* AND I HAD **NO IDEA.**

YOU KNOW HOW MUCH *HOCKEY* MEANS TO ME!

I THOUGHT YOU DIDN'T CARE.

YOU THOUGHT I DIDN'T CARE.

AND MOM CERTAINLY NEVER-- WAIT, DOES *MOM* EVEN KNOW?

I--

OH MY GOSH. I CAN'T *BELIEVE* YOU WERE A MEGASTAR BETWEEN THE PIPES!

THIS IS THE *MOST AWESOME* THING IN MY ENTIRE *LIFE!* DID YOU START WHEN YOU WERE LITTLE? WERE YOU ALWAYS A GOALIE? DID YOU WEAR ONE OF THOSE COOL RETRO MASKS LIKE THE ONES THEY GAVE OUT AT MY TOURNAMENT LAST YEAR?

WHY DIDN'T YOU TELL ME, GRANDMA? DID SOMETHING *HAPPEN?* WHY--?

I THINK WE'D BETTER HOLD OFF ON THE PASTA.

"I PLAYED FOR A COUPLE OF YEARS WITH NO PROBLEM, BUT THEN I GOT *CAUGHT* WHILE I WAS ON THE PROVISIONAL ALL-STAR TEAM.

"WE WERE SUPPOSED TO PLAY IN THE *CANADIAN U14 CHAMPIONSHIPS...*

"... BUT THE TEAM WE WERE PLAYING FROM TORONTO THOUGHT I MUST HAVE BEEN SIXTEEN OR SEVENTEEN...

"... BECAUSE I HADN'T GIVEN UP A *GOAL* ALL TOURNAMENT. *NOT ONE!*

"THEN THEY CHECKED MY SCHOOL RECORDS AND FOUND OUT I WAS LISTED AS *JOSEPHINE CAMERON.* THEY PROTESTED, AND I GOT KICKED OFF THE TEAM."

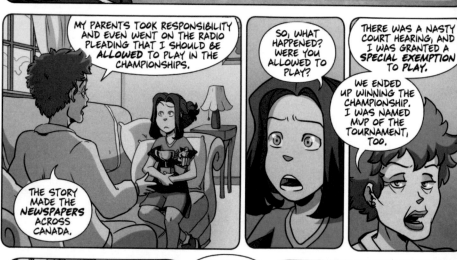

MY PARENTS TOOK RESPONSIBILITY AND EVEN WENT ON THE RADIO PLEADING THAT I SHOULD BE *ALLOWED* TO PLAY IN THE CHAMPIONSHIPS.

THE STORY MADE THE *NEWSPAPERS* ACROSS CANADA.

SO, WHAT HAPPENED? WERE YOU ALLOWED TO PLAY?

THERE WAS A NASTY COURT HEARING, AND I WAS GRANTED A *SPECIAL EXEMPTION* TO PLAY.

WE ENDED UP WINNING THE CHAMPIONSHIP. I WAS NAMED MVP OF THE TOURNAMENT, TOO.

GIRL POWER! YOU SHOWED THEM!

I SHOWED THEM, BUT THE COURT BATTLE AND ALL THE *ANGRY* PEOPLE WRITING TO THE NEWSPAPERS OR SHOUTING AT US FROM THE BLEACHERS...

... CAUSED A LOT OF *STRESS* FOR ME, MY PARENTS, AND MY TEAMMATES, WHO GOT CAUGHT IN THE MIDDLE.

PLAYING AS A TEAM GOT *COMPLICATED.* WE DIDN'T TRUST EACH OTHER ANYMORE, I GUESS...

... OR MAYBE THE *NEGATIVITY* ON THE OUTSIDE MANAGED TO SEEP ONTO THE HOCKEY RINK, TOO.

ALL I WANTED TO DO WAS PLAY THE GAME I *LOVED* SO MUCH--IT WAS SUCH A SIMPLE THING THAT TURNED INTO A *MESS.* SO, I LEFT THE TEAM.

BUT... I MEAN, YOU WON IN COURT!

YOU'RE THINKING *"QUITTER,"* RIGHT?

IT'S DIFFICULT TO EXPLAIN.

I COULDN'T PLAY ON MY HOME TEAM ANYMORE-- WE HAD SO MUCH TO WORK THROUGH THAT IT WOULD'VE BEEN *IMPOSSIBLE* TO FOCUS ON PLAYING OUR BEST GAME TOGETHER. I DECIDED TO PLAY AGAINST *GIRLS* INSTEAD, SO WE MADE THE LONG DRIVE BACK AND FORTH TO THE NEAREST GIRLS' LEAGUE.

THE COMPETITION WASN'T THERE, AND I GUESS...

...THERE WERE TOO MANY BAD MEMORIES.

IT SIMPLY *WASN'T FUN* FOR ME ANYMORE. SO I HUNG UP MY SKATES AND THAT WAS THAT.

THAT WAS IT? YOU *NEVER* PLAYED AGAIN?

THAT WAS IT.

BUT YOU...

...DON'T YOU EVER WISH...?

I DID FOR A LONG TIME--I SECOND-GUESSED MYSELF EVERY DAY. SHOULD I HAVE STAYED OR NOT? SHOULD I HAVE *MADE WAVES* OR NOT? EVEN AFTERWARD, PEOPLE CALLED ME A TROUBLEMAKER, AND THAT WAS HARD TO LIVE WITH. FOR A WHILE I WAS *SORRY* I'D TRIED SO HARD TO PLAY. THEN I WAS SORRY I *STOPPED.*

I'VE *LEARNED* TO LIVE WITH THE REGRET, BUT THE SHAME YOU NEVER LOSE. IT'S JUST... VERY *COMPLICATED,* LIKE I SAID.

I GUESS THAT'S WHY YOU DIDN'T TALK TO ANYONE ABOUT IT.

CHAPTER 9

WELL, AFTER *THAT*, I CERTAINLY WASN'T COMING BACK TO TENNESSEE.

THE NEXT DAY, GRANDMA DIDN'T SAY A WORD WHEN I CAME DOWNSTAIRS DRESSED AND READY TO GO.

SHE JUST MADE BACON AND EGGS AND DROVE ME TO CAMP LIKE NORMAL. BUT SHE GAVE ME A THUMBS-UP WHEN SHE DROPPED ME OFF, SO I THINK MAYBE SHE WAS PROUD OF ME.

BESIDES, DECIDING TO COME BACK WAS THE EASY PART.

NOW IT WAS TIME TO TALK TO COACH THATCHER.

THE SECOND I WALKED INTO CAMP THAT DAY, I KNEW I WOULD'VE REGRETTED GOING HOME.

YOU HEAR PEOPLE TALKING ABOUT THE **GOOD OLD DAYS,** BUT THERE WAS **NOTHING GOOD** ABOUT WHAT HAPPENED TO GRANDMA BACK THEN.

I COULDN'T IMAGINE QUITTING HOCKEY ALTOGETHER--LIKE GRANDMA DID.

JUST BECAUSE SHE WAS A **GIRL** WHO WANTED TO **COMPETE** IN A GAME SHE LOVED AND WAS **REALLY GOOD** AT.

SHE JUST WANTED TO BE RESPECTED AND TREATED EQUALLY.

I COULDN'T UNDERSTAND WHY SHE WASN'T ANGRY.

I CERTAINLY WAS.

I COULDN'T FIX JOCELYN AND I COULDN'T FIX SARAH. I COULDN'T FIX THE FACT THAT COACH THATCHER LIKED THEM BETTER.

BUT I SURE AS HECK WAS GOING TO FIX **SOMETHING,** AND THAT WAS GRANDMA BEING FORCED OFF THE ICE.

WHICH GAVE ME AN IDEA.

COA

I MUST SAY I'M SURPRISED TO SEE YOU BACK HERE, KATE. I THOUGHT YOU'D BE ON YOUR WAY HOME TO TENNESSEE THIS MORNING.

I ALMOST WAS.

MY GRANDMA, SHE WAS--WELL, I MEAN, WE TALKED.

AND I WANTED TO **APOLOGIZE** FOR MY BEHAVIOR YESTERDAY. I'M GOING TO FOCUS ON MY GAME AND TAKE IN AS MUCH FROM YOU AND COACH ROSSETTI AS I CAN.

APOLOGY ACCEPTED. IT'S GOOD TO HEAR YOU'RE COMMITTED TO LEARNING AND **IMPROVING** YOURSELF AS A PLAYER AND AS A PERSON.

YES? ANYTHING ELSE?

OKAY, KATE, LET'S DO THIS.

...

UH... NO! THANK YOU, COACH!

I'D PLANNED TO ASK COACH TO LET GRANDMA COME SHOW US HER MAD GOALTENDING SKILLS.

GRANDMA'S DREAM WHEN SHE WAS MY AGE WAS TO REPRESENT CANADA IN THE OLYMPICS SOMEDAY, EVEN THOUGH THERE WASN'T A WOMEN'S EVENT AT THE TIME. AND COACH THATCHER AND COACH ROSSETTI WERE BOTH OLYMPIANS. I HAD IT ALL FIGURED OUT.

BUT COACH THATCHER WASN'T EXACTLY ON MY SIDE, AND I REALLY DIDN'T WANT TO BLOW GRANDMA'S CHANCES.

I FIGURED I'D PROVE TO THE COACHES THAT I WAS SERIOUS ABOUT THE GAME AND THEN ASK FOR FAVORS.

PLUS, I NEEDED TO SHOW JOCELYN A THING OR TWO.

THE REST OF THE WEEK WENT A LOT BETTER.

I'D DECIDED I WAS THERE TO BE A PLAYER THE COACHES COULD TRUST WHEN IT REALLY MATTERED.

PUSH

JOCELYN WAS COMMITTED.

BUT SO WAS I.

KATE, I'M **PROUD** OF YOU FOR STICKING IT OUT--AND COMING BACK EVEN STRONGER.

YOU MAY NOT BELIEVE THIS, BUT WHEN I WAS YOUR AGE, I HAD SOME TROUBLE OF MY OWN WHEN A RIVAL GOT IN MY FACE.

IT TOOK A COACH WHO MAKES COACH THATCHER LOOK SHY TO STRAIGHTEN ME OUT, AND I ENDED UP WITH A REAL CHANCE AT MY DREAM.

I KNOW THAT IF YOU WORK HARD AND PUSH YOURSELF TO HEIGHTS YOU DIDN'T THINK YOU COULD REACH, YOU CAN BECOME A **WORLD-CLASS HOCKEY PLAYER**, BOTH ON AND OFF THE ICE.

FINALLY, SOMEONE WAS NOTICING!

THE EVENINGS AFTER CAMP WERE EVEN BETTER.

'NIGHT, GRANDMA!

BZZ

MOM...

WELL, MOSTLY.

I HADN'T TOLD MOM I KNEW ABOUT GRANDMA'S HOCKEY HISTORY YET.

I'D ASKED GRANDMA NOT TO SAY ANYTHING EITHER--

--TO LET ME TALK TO *MOM* ABOUT IT FIRST.

EXCEPT I WASN'T SURE EXACTLY HOW TO START.

Hey!

HOW ABOUT, "HEY MOM, MY DAY WENT GREAT! I JUST FOUND OUT YOU KEPT THIS HUGE SECRET FROM ME ABOUT MY *GRANDMOTHER* THAT BASICALLY STOPPED ME FROM HAVING A *RELATIONSHIP* WITH HER, LIKE EVER! AND YOU ALSO LET ME THINK GRANDMA DIDN'T *CARE* ABOUT ME OR WHAT WAS *IMPORTANT* IN MY LIFE--

"--EVEN WHEN I TOLD YOU WE HAD NOTHING IN COMMON! SO... WHAT *OTHER SECRETS* ARE YOU HIDING FROM ME?"

YEAH, NOPE.

KIND OF COMPLICATED WHEN YOU'RE TWELVE HUNDRED MILES AWAY.

BZZ BZZ

How was today?

Good.

Hey!

How was today?

Good.

I mean...

Great!

JUST THE USUAL HOCKEY STUFF.

OH, AND DEALING WITH FAMILY SECRETS...

...PLUS I NEED TO SHOW UP TWO BULLIES, BEAT THEM IN THE END-OF-CAMP TOURNAMENT...

...PROVE TO THE COACHES I CAN PLAY JUST AS WELL AS ANY OF THE GIRLS...

...STOP BEING **SCARED STIFF** OF COACH THATCHER...

...AND FIGURE OUT A WAY TO GET GRANDMA OUT OF **RETIREMENT** AND PLAYING HOCKEY AGAIN...

CHAPTER 10

I JUST KNEW WE'D CRUSH IT IN THE TOURNAMENT!

KATE, DID YOU HEAR? COACH THATCHER'S CHANGING UP THE UNITS FOR THE TOURNAMENT.

NO WAY!

COME ON! THE TOURNAMENT ASSIGNMENTS ARE UP!

OOOH!

!

UNIT 3

NAYELI

KATE

JOCELYN

UNIT 4

ANYA

NIKO

CAYLA

I MIGHT HAVE **FREAKED OUT** JUST A LITTLE.

IT'S JUST FOR THE TOURNAMENT.

AND SHE'LL BE ON YOUR TEAM. SHE WANTS TO **WIN!** WHY WOULD SHE MESS WITH YOU?

THE TOURNAMENT DOESN'T START TILL TOMORROW ANYWAY, AND **RIGHT NOW** WE HAVE A GAME TO PLAY.

OKAY, OKAY. SORRY.

GET YOUR HEAD IN THE **GAME,** NAYELI.

I'D BEEN PLAYING BETTER WITH NAYELI AND PRISHA BECAUSE WE WERE FINALLY **FOCUSED** ON **EACH OTHER,** RATHER THAN ME WORRYING ABOUT JOCELYN AND MY FRIENDS WORRYING ABOUT ME.

NOW I WAS **DISTRACTING** NAYELI WITH MY DRAMA **AGAIN**--AND THAT WASN'T FAIR TO MY BEST FRIEND AND TEAMMATE.

THE NEXT DAY...

WE NEED TO TALK.

THERE WAS ONLY ONE WAY TO GET THROUGH THIS TOURNAMENT.

WE'RE NOT FRIENDS, BUT IT DOESN'T MATTER. WE HAVE TO WORK TOGETHER, OR WE DON'T HAVE A CHANCE AT WINNING.

AND I WANTED TO GO OUT A WINNER.

...

FINE. LET'S DO THIS.

#3   1:42   #4
3   4

#3   1:12   #4
3   5

EASIER SAID THAN DONE.

GRR!

WHAT WERE YOU DOING OUT THERE?!

YOU SHOULD HAVE BEEN COVERING THE SHOOTER!

I WAS COVERING HER, BUT THEN I GOT PICKED BY ANYA AND TOLD YOU TO SWITCH, BUT YOU JUST STAYED WITH NIKO!

YOU YELLED IT TOO LATE, AND I DIDN'T HAVE ENOUGH TIME TO GET OVER THERE! THAT'S ON YOU!

ENOUGH!!

WE LOST THE GAME, FINE! BUT WE'RE GOING TO LOSE A LOT MORE GAMES IF YOU TWO DON'T STOP BLAMING EACH OTHER.

I DIDN'T TRAVEL THOUSANDS OF MILES JUST TO LISTEN TO YOU FIGHT LIKE STRAY CATS...

... WHILE WE KEEP LOSING BECAUSE YOU CAN'T GET IT TOGETHER!

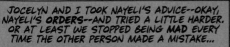

JOCELYN AND I TOOK NAYELI'S ADVICE--OKAY, NAYELI'S *ORDERS*--AND TRIED A LITTLE HARDER. OR AT LEAST WE STOPPED BEING *MAD* EVERY TIME THE OTHER PERSON MADE A *MISTAKE...*

... WHICH MEANT WE ENDED UP MAKING A LOT *FEWER* MISTAKES.

BUT NOT FEW ENOUGH MISTAKES TO START *WINNING.*

I WAS TRYING. NAYELI WAS TRYING. JOCELYN WAS TRYING. HONESTLY. BUT WE WERE TOO MUCH LIKE GRANDMA'S TEAM AFTER HER COURT CASE.

GRANDMA SAID THEY *STOPPED TRUSTING* EACH OTHER, WHICH MEANT THEY COULDN'T WORK *TOGETHER* AS A *TEAM* ANYMORE.

THAT DIDN'T SOUND GOOD FOR ME AND JOCELYN, BECAUSE I WAS PRETTY SURE WE'D NEVER TRUST EACH OTHER.

KATE?

GREAT. JUST WHAT I NEEDED.

TOUGH GAME, BUT WAY TO GRIND IT OUT. KEEP UP THAT KIND OF EFFORT AND INTENSITY, AND YOU'LL COME OUT ON TOP MORE OFTEN THAN NOT.

FROM COACH THATCHER THAT WAS PRACTICALLY AN OLYMPIC MEDAL. SHE WAS ACTUALLY *SMILING!*

COACH WAS IN A GOOD MOOD, WHICH MEANT IT WAS *NOW OR NEVER.*

KNOCK

COACH

COACH THATCHER, COACH ROSSETTI? I WANTED TO ASK YOU BOTH FOR A HUGE *FAVOR.* I KNOW CAMP'S OVER NEXT WEEK, BUT... UM...

THIS ISN'T ABOUT THE TOURNAMENT ASSIGNMENTS, IS IT?

NO, NO!

IT'S ABOUT MY *GRANDMOTHER.*

I'M ABSOLUTELY **HONORED** YOU ASKED ME.

KATE, IT WILL DEPEND ON HOW SHE **FEELS.** REMEMBER THAT YOUR GRANDMOTHER IS ALMOST SEVENTY YEARS OLD.

ACTUALLY, SIXTY-EIGHT AND THREE QUARTERS.

MOM SEEMED WAY LESS PLEASED THAN I EXPECTED.

I'M SORRY, MOM, BUT I WANT TO EMPHASIZE TO KATE THAT YOU HAVE **LIMITS.**

YOU'VE GOT TO STOP PUSHING YOURSELF!

SHE KEPT BRINGING IT UP ALL EVENING.

SO WHAT WOULD YOU HAVE ME DO? JUST SIT HERE ON THE COUCH UNTIL I CRUMBLE AWAY INTO **DUST?**

I'M NOT SAYING THAT AT ALL! BUT YOU HAVE TO **TAKE CARE OF** YOURSELF.

I DIDN'T KNOW WHY SHE WAS MAKING SUCH A **BIG DEAL** OF IT.

I SURE FOUND OUT LATER.

I SHOULD HAVE TOLD HER THE FIRST TIME YOU HAD **BREAST CANCER.** THAT WAS MY MISTAKE. I MADE IT WORSE BY NOT TELLING HER YOU BEAT IT.

NOW THAT IT'S **BACK,** I JUST...

WHAT?!

OH, KATE.

HONEY--

MORE *SECRETS?* WHEN ARE YOU GOING TO *STOP* TREATING ME LIKE A *KID* AND *TELL* ME ABOUT THE STUFF THAT *REALLY* MATTERS?!

SLAM

CHAPTER 11

kNOCK
kNOCK

HI, GRANDMA. COME IN.

YOUR MOM AND I ARE...

...BOTH **VERY SORRY** THAT WE DIDN'T TELL YOU ABOUT EITHER CANCER DIAGNOSIS. WE DIDN'T... WE DIDN'T KNOW HOW YOU'D **HANDLE** IT.

THAT WAS **WRONG** OF US. WE SHOULD HAVE **TRUSTED** YOU.

BECAUSE YOU'RE RIGHT--THIS IS WHAT **REALLY** MATTERS.

YOU AND I DIDN'T KNOW EACH OTHER THAT WELL BEFORE YOU CAME OUT HERE. I'M GLAD THAT'S **CHANGED**...

...AND THAT MY HOCKEY SECRET'S NOT SO **SECRET** ANYMORE!

AND KATE, IT MATTERS **TO ME** WHAT'S GOING ON IN YOUR **WORLD**, TOO.

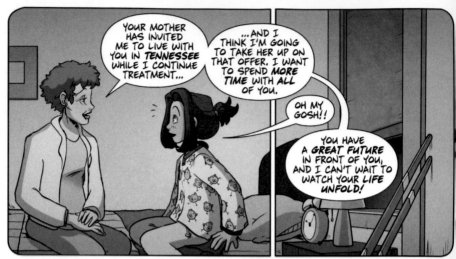

YOUR MOTHER HAS INVITED ME TO LIVE WITH YOU IN *TENNESSEE* WHILE I CONTINUE TREATMENT...

...AND I THINK I'M GOING TO TAKE HER UP ON THAT OFFER. I WANT TO SPEND *MORE TIME* WITH *ALL* OF YOU.

OH MY GOSH!!

YOU HAVE A *GREAT FUTURE* IN FRONT OF YOU, AND I CAN'T WAIT TO WATCH YOUR *LIFE UNFOLD!*

I CAN'T BELIEVE I *ALMOST QUIT* CAMP BECAUSE THINGS WEREN'T GOING MY WAY.

BUT YOU DIDN'T LEAVE, *DID* YOU?

BECAUSE *YOU* TALKED ME OUT OF IT!

I JUST TOLD YOU MY STORY. IT WAS UP TO YOU TO *DECIDE* WHAT YOU WANTED TO DO WITH IT. YOU *STAYED* AND *PROSPERED,* AND YOU SHOWED REAL CLASS.

NOT TO MENTION MASTERMINDING A PLAN TO GET ME *BACK ON THE ICE!*

NOW WHY DON'T YOU TELL ME ALL ABOUT IT?

THE NEXT DAY WAS WEIRD.

I DIDN'T KNOW WHETHER TO BE EXCITED--GRANDMA WAS COMING TO LIVE WITH US!--

--OR SCARED BECAUSE GRANDMA WAS SICK.

BUT GRANDMA COULDN'T WAIT TO PLAY WITH US AT THE END OF CAMP, AND THE OTHER GIRLS WERE TOTALLY PUMPED.

PLUS, I WAS STILL MAD AT MOM ABOUT EVERYTHING.

I KNEW I WAS ACTING LIKE A LITTLE KID, BUT I WASN'T READY TO TALK TO HER YET. I GUESS I WAS JUST CONFUSED ALL AROUND.

SO WHEN COACH ROSSETTI ASKED ME IF EVERYTHING WAS OKAY...

:SNIFF:

...I JUST COULDN'T HOLD IT IN. I TOLD HER ABOUT GRANDMA'S DIAGNOSIS.

YOUR MOM CALLED THIS MORNING TO LET US KNOW. YOUR GRANDMA'S A FIGHTER...

... BUT IT'S OKAY TO SAY THAT THIS SUCKS.

THERE WILL BE TIMES BOTH ON AND OFF THE ICE THAT WILL TEST YOU...

... AND THIS IS ONE OF THEM. YOUR GRANDMA'S GOING TO NEED YOUR LOVE AND SUPPORT. I KNOW YOU'LL HAVE HER BACK, RIGHT?

I SURE WILL.

...

UM, KATE? I HEARD COACH THATCHER AND COACH ROSSETTI TALKING ABOUT YOUR GRANDMOTHER.

SO SHE *DOES* KNOW MY NAME.

I THOUGHT JOCELYN WANTED TO BE MY BFF NOW THAT SHE'D FOUND OUT GRANDMA WAS A HOCKEY ICON.

ABOUT HER HAVING CANCER. I... MY *AUNT* HAD CANCER TWO YEARS AGO...

...AND IT WAS *REALLY HARD* ON MY FAMILY. I'M REALLY *CLOSE* WITH MY AUNT. SHE'S LIKE A SECOND MOM TO ME.

I GUESS I WANTED TO SAY THAT I'M *SORRY* YOUR GRANDMA'S SICK. I *HOPE* SHE RECOVERS REALLY FAST.

ALSO, UM, I'M SORRY FOR BEING A...*YOU KNOW*...HERE AT CAMP. AND FOR BLAMING YOU FOR OUR UNIT LOSING.

I ACTUALLY THINK YOU'RE PRETTY *AWESOME* OUT THERE.

SO ARE YOU! AND, UM, I'M **SORRY** FOR WHAT I DID A FEW WEEKS AGO. THAT WASN'T COOL.

UNIT 3, UNIT 4, YOU'RE **UP!**

PUFF PUFF

WHIIIIZ

FIIIIII

IT WAS A HECK OF A LOT MORE FUN...

...WORKING WITH JOCELYN...

TAK

...THAN TRYING TO STEAMROLL EACH OTHER.

TEK

TOCK

I'M PROUDER OF YOUR TEAMWORK THAN I WOULD'VE BEEN IF YOU'D WON THE TOURNAMENT.

AFTER THAT, I FELT LIKE I COULD CONQUER THE WORLD...OR AT LEAST PART OF THE WORLD.

MY PART OF THE WORLD.

CHAPTER 12

I'M ALMOST *THIRTEEN!*

ACT MATURE, ACT MATURE.

I'M NOT A LITTLE KID ANYMORE, MOM. LIFE GETS *SERIOUS* SOMETIMES...

...AND I DON'T NEED TO BE PROTECTED FROM THAT.

AND I CAN HANDLE A BIT OF SERIOUSNESS JUST FINE. GRANDMA WAS JUST A LITTLE OLDER THAN ME WHEN SHE STOOD UP AGAINST *DISCRIMINATION* AND WON THE RIGHT TO PLAY WITH THE BOYS.

I STILL CAN'T BELIEVE YOU KNOW ABOUT THAT.

YEAH, I KNOW... I KEPT A SECRET, TOO.

I WASN'T SURE HOW TO TALK ABOUT IT OVER THE PHONE WITHOUT GETTING MAD AT YOU, AND THEN... THERE WAS SO MUCH I WANTED TO SAY, BUT I WASN'T SURE *HOW* TO SAY IT.

MY NOT TELLING YOU ABOUT GRANDMA'S CANCER WAS A LITTLE LIKE THAT, TOO. I'M HAVING A TOUGH TIME WITH IT, AND SHE DIDN'T TELL ME MUCH ABOUT HER ILLNESS THE FIRST TIME, SO I'VE BEEN FEELING A LITTLE... *LOST.*

IT WASN'T FAIR TO *ASSUME* YOU WOULD REACT THE SAME WAY.

GRANDMA DIDN'T TELL YOU ABOUT BEING SICK THE FIRST TIME?

NOT UNTIL PARTWAY THROUGH THE TREATMENT, NO.

WOW.

YEAH.

YOU MUST HAVE FREAKED.

I MOST CERTAINLY DID.

I COULDN'T BELIEVE GRANDMA HADN'T TOLD MOM WHEN SHE HAD CANCER THE FIRST TIME.

MOMS AND DAUGHTERS ARE COMPLICATED, AREN'T THEY?

I GUESS WE ALL KEPT SECRETS FOR DIFFERENT REASONS, BUT THE LONGER WE KEPT THEM, THE HARDER IT WAS TO TALK TO EACH OTHER AT ALL.

I NEED TO TELL YOU ABOUT HOW I ALMOST QUIT CAMP.

IT FELT SO GOOD TO FINALLY TALK TO MOM ABOUT CAMP, ABOUT JOCELYN, ABOUT EVERYTHING.

TWO HOURS LATER...

HELLO, YOU TWO.

I JUST GOT OFF THE PHONE WITH COACH ROSSETTI. I CAN'T BELIEVE HOW WELL YOU ORCHESTRATED MY COMEBACK.

APPARENTLY YOU DESCRIBED ME AS THE G.O.A.T.?

GREATEST OF ALL TIME!

FROM WHAT THE COACH SAID, IT SOUNDS LIKE YOU'RE GETTING THERE YOURSELF.

WHICH IS ONE OF THE REASONS I TOOK OUT THIS OLD HAT.

I HAVEN'T THOUGHT ABOUT THIS THING IN YEARS.

"WHEN I WAS GROWING UP, THE KIDS IN MY NEIGHBORHOOD WOULD PLAY ON A FROZEN POND NEAR THE EDGE OF TOWN. I WASN'T THE GOALIE WHEN WE STARTED PLAYING...

"...THAT CAME LATER. AND I WAS ALWAYS COLD, SO MY MOM KNITTED ME THIS HAT--*ORANGE*, MY FAVORITE COLOR.

"ONCE I STARTED PLAYING GOALIE, I WORE IT ON TOP OF MY MASK AS A SORT OF *GOOD-LUCK CHARM*. THIS HAT WAS WITH ME AT *EVERY* GAME-- INCLUDING THE GAMES WHERE I EARNED THOSE TROPHIES YOU SAW.

"ESPECIALLY THOSE GAMES."

I HAD IT WITH ME DURING THE COURT HEARING, TOO. BUT AFTER THAT, I PACKED IT UP ALONG WITH MY STICKS AND MASK.

NOW... WELL, I SHOULD HAVE MY LUCKY HAT WITH ME FOR MY *HOCKEY COMEBACK*.

BESIDES, I FIGURED THE *WIG* WOULDN'T TAKE WELL TO THE EQUIPMENT COACH ROSSETTI HAS READY FOR ME, SO--

WIG?!

NO MORE SECRETS.

DURING THE COURT HEARING, IT ALSO BECAME A WAY FOR ME TO *HIDE*. I WOULD *PULL IT* OVER MY EYES.

BUT I DIDN'T NEED TO HIDE WHO I *WAS*, OR ANYTHING ABOUT ME. NOT FROM THE PEOPLE BACK THEN AND *NOT FROM MY FAMILY* NOW.

I ONLY NEED TO WORRY ABOUT KEEPING MY *EARS WARM*.

NEXT WEEK I'LL WEAR THE HAT ON THE ICE AGAIN, BUT ONCE I *REALLY GO INTO* RETIREMENT, THE HAT'S *YOURS*, KATE.

FOR YEARS, I'VE WANTED YOU TO BE PART OF MY HOCKEY STORY. AND SINCE YOU'RE GIVING ME A CHANCE TO *REWRITE THE ENDING--* WELL, IT'S PERFECT, ISN'T IT?

CHAPTER 13

WHEN CAMP ENDED THAT WEEK, IT WAS TOUGH TO SAY GOODBYE TO MY NEW FRIENDS, BUT WE SET UP A HUGE *CHAT GROUP* AND WE'RE ON THERE EVERY DAY.

EVEN JOCELYN, WHO, WELL... SHE CAN STILL BE SNARKY, BUT SHE'S NOT LIKE SHE USED TO BE.

AND NAYELI AND PRISHA ARE AS AWESOME AS EVER.

I HOPE THEY COME BACK TO THE U.S. SOMEDAY... OR MAYBE I CAN *VISIT* THEM!

A FEW WEEKS AFTER CAMP, DAD AND DUSTIN AND I DROVE BACK OUT TO COLORADO TO HELP *MOVE* GRANDMA *HERE* TO TENNESSEE.

SHE'S STAYING FOR A FEW MONTHS, MAYBE LONGER. I THINK MOM SECRETLY WANTS HER TO MOVE OUT HERE FOR GOOD, BUT GRANDMA'S PRETTY *INDEPENDENT.*

SHE'S HERE *NOW?*

ACTUALLY... SHE'S COMING TO PICK ME UP THIS AFTERNOON.

CAN I *MEET* HER?

HONK HONK HONK HONK

READY FOR HOCKEY PRACTICE?

I EVEN HAVE MY LUCKY HAT.

Acknowledgments

CMF: Howard Shapiro, writing this with you was an absolute blast, and I couldn't have asked for a better or more supportive dynamic from start to finish. Thank you for listening to every single idea, even the crazy ones, and for being patient when I insisted that this revision was absolutely, I promise, the very last time I changed a scene. (Speaking of which…)

To Jade Gonzalez, Lizz Buenaventura, and Saida Temofonte: You all are artistic rock stars, and with the way you brought Kate and her world to life, I'm pretty sure you're wizards or magicians too. Thank you for your incredible work and creativity. I love how your vision became part of every scene.

Molly McCowan: It takes a special kind of person to edit an editor. Thank you for being classy all the way, and *wow*, did you ever make some good catches. ::grins embarrassedly:: And Heidi Ward, I'm grateful, too, for your sharp eye and your ability to spot the tiny things that totally escaped my notice.

Adam Frey, you've been my number one cheerleader from the start—not to mention a walking comics encyclopedia. I never had an art, layout, or storytelling question you couldn't answer (but I'll keep trying). Your support has meant everything to me.

To Kiersten Frey, a.k.a. Viola Girl: This book couldn't have happened without your boundless enthusiasm and your keen eye for detail. Thanks especially for the many times you suggested changes because "No one's used that word since like 2006, except for parents who are trying to look cool." But seriously: *Did I look cool?*

And finally, to Mémé and Nana: Thank you for always being proud of me. I'm lucky to have had such wonderful grandmothers.

HS: Thanks to all my friends at Animal Inc. and Animal Media Group, LLC. You made this possible, and for that I will always be appreciative! Thank you so much, Brianne Halverson, for being a fantastic publicist and a better friend. Thanks to Chizz Communications (Olivia, Vlad, David, and Jermaine) for your marketing help and support, and thanks to everyone at Consortium Book Sales and Distribution for all you do to get our books into the marketplace.

A huge thank you to Kendall Coyne, Marie-Philip Poulin, and Hayley Wickenheiser for taking the time to read Kate's story and provide such wonderful endorsements. It means a great deal!

Special thanks to our all-star creative team—the great, great Jade Gonzalez, Lizz Buenaventura, Saida Temofonte, Pilar Brown, and Kiersten Frey—for your creativity, vision, and hard work bringing this story to life. Jade, thank you for doing such a tremendous job illustrating the book. You were an absolute joy to work with, and we're grateful for your unbelievable dedication and work ethic. Lizz, you have been with the project from the start—without you it would not exist. Thanks for bringing Jade on board and for being so singularly dedicated! I have my colorist for life in you! Saida, you are an absolute rock star letterer and the book's secret weapon. Thanks for adding so much to the story. Pilar, thank you for being unflappable and always keeping the straight-ahead purpose of getting our books off to the printer under very tight (i.e., crazy) deadlines. Thank you, Kiersten, for being the project's overall sounding board. Your time, help, and input have been tremendously appreciated.

Very special thanks to Christina M. Frey for being such a wonderful creative partner in Kate's journey. Simply put, you saved the project and helped make it better than I could have ever imagined. I hope we have many more Kate stories to tell in the future!

Christina M. Frey grew up writing stories in her head and on every available surface, even when her teacher told her that language arts was over and it was time to focus on something else. Now she works as a developmental editor, helping other storytellers turn their ideas into books of their own. At night she reads for fun, writes her own stories, and ends up going to bed way too late. Christina lives in Maryland with her husband and daughter and their three hermit crabs. Find her online at www.cmfreywrites.com.

Howard Shapiro lives in Moon Township, Pennsylvania, with his wife and two sons. The controller for the Pittsburgh-based visual effects firm Animal Inc., he has written nine other books; *Kate's Really Good at Hockey* is his fifth hockey-themed book.

In 2010 Howard launched a corporate sponsorship program that to date has donated 2,500 of his children's hockey books to NHL teams for their community and educational initiatives. Since 2006 his annual charity raffle, which he matches dollar for dollar, has raised funds for hockey-related charities, including the Mario Lemieux Foundation and Hockey Fights Cancer. For more information, email hockeyplayer4life@gmail.com.